THE ORPHAN AND THE DOLL

by Tracy Friedman

Illustrated by
Emily Arnold McCully

A
LITTLE APPLE
PAPERBACK

SCHOLASTIC INC.

New York   Toronto   London   Auckland   Sydney

ISBN 0-590-41369-4

Copyright © 1988 by Tracy Friedman.
Illustrations copyright © 1988 by Scholastic Books, Inc.
All rights reserved. Published by Scholastic Inc. APPLE PAPERBACKS is a registered trademark of Scholastic Inc.

12 11 10 9 8 7 6 5 4 3 2 1   8 9/8 0 1 2 3/9

Printed in the U.S.A.   28

First Scholastic printing, November 1988

ALSO AVAILABLE FROM SCHOLASTIC:

Henriette: The Story of a Doll
by Tracy Friedman

Chapter One

WHEN Amanda woke up and found a beautiful china doll at the foot of her bed, she thought she was dreaming. She closed her eyes and held them shut for a long time. But when she opened them again, the doll was still there. Her head was tilted thoughtfully to one side, and her graceful hands were lifted in the air as if she were about to speak.

The doll was wearing a sky-blue satin gown that was torn and muddy. One of her pink satin slippers was missing. She had smudges of dirt on her cheeks and chin, but even this could not hide her beauty. Her bright blue eyes and painted rosebud mouth had a softness that only time can bring. Her lovely porcelain face seemed wise and kind. Amanda had never seen this doll before, yet something about the expression on her face made Amanda feel that they had known each other all their lives.

"What's her name?" asked Molly. Molly was the girl who slept in the bed next to Amanda.

Without even pausing to think, Amanda answered, "Henriette. Her name is Henriette."

"How do you know?" asked Molly.

"I'm not sure. But her name *is* Henriette. I know it just as surely as I know that my name is Amanda."

By this time two other girls, Rachel and Emily, had gotten out of bed and come over to look at the doll.

"How did she get here?" asked Rachel. Rachel was much taller than the other girls. She tended to be bossy and unpleasant.

"I don't know how she got here," said Amanda. "But I think she came to bring me back my locket." It was only at that very moment Amanda realized her locket was securely fastened around her neck. It was a tiny gold locket on a fine gold chain. Inside were two miniature portraits. One was a picture of Amanda herself when she was very small. The other was a picture of a handsome young man in a military uniform. Amanda believed that the man was her father. She had never known her father or her mother. They had all gotten separated a long time ago during the War Between the States. Amanda had worn the locket around her neck ever since she could remember.

"I thought Mrs. Crabtree took your locket weeks ago," said Rachel.

"She did," said Amanda. "But somehow Henriette got hold of it. And now she has brought it back to me."

"That's silly!" said Rachel. "Come on, Emily. Amanda's making up stories again. And it's nearly time for breakfast."

Rachel and Emily walked away, leaving Amanda and Molly alone with the doll. Just then a bell rang. "You'd better hurry," said Molly as she ran off to get washed.

Amanda threw back the covers and hopped out of bed. She took her shoes and stockings out of the cupboard and put them on. She wiggled out of her nightgown and stepped into a gray flannel dress that buttoned up the front. Breakfast at the orphanage was served promptly at eight A.M. and no one was allowed to be late.

When Amanda finished dressing, she made her bed quickly, closed the cupboard, and headed for the door. All the other children had already gone down to the dining room. The breakfast bell rang again, and yet Amanda didn't want to go. She paused in the doorway with a worried expression on her face, then turned back to look at Henriette.

The doll was sitting quietly at the foot of the bed. Amanda could hear the faraway sounds of the other children at breakfast. A bird was singing somewhere out-of-doors, and in the distance a dog was barking. Suddenly a smile crept across Amanda's face. For in the midst of all the other sounds she seemed to hear a doll-like voice whisper, "Do not fear, you are my mistress now. I belong to you and you belong to me. I will be here when you return."

Amanda turned and ran happily off to breakfast.

Chapter Two

As soon as Amanda's footsteps had died away, Henriette folded her hands in her lap and sighed a very small sigh. It was a sigh of pure contentment. As far as Henriette was concerned it was a wonderful day. Now that she had found her rightful mistress, what could be wrong in the world?

It was just about then that she sneezed. As a matter of fact she sneezed twice. "Good gracious," said Henriette to herself. "I hope I have not caught cold." She reached into the pocket of her hoopskirt to find her handkerchief, but instead pulled out one very dirty white kid glove.

Tiens, thought Henriette, who had come

from France, and often spoke French to herself when she was alone. How could this have happened? But then she remembered. She had spoiled her best white gloves while trying to climb into a basket of cotton. That was many days ago, at the beginning of her journey.

Henriette had come a long way to find Amanda. She had traveled nearly one hundred miles, all the way across the state of Georgia, from a plantation in the country to the city of Atlanta.

And what a journey it had been. Henriette had come by train, by coach, and on foot. She had lost her way, then found it again. She had been tired and cold and wet and hungry. But the thought of finding Amanda always pushed her on.

Henriette continued to rummage in her pocket and finally found her handkerchief. She blew her nose and decided it was time to do something about her appearance. Henriette had been so tired when she arrived at the orphanage late the night before, she had simply put her head on Amanda's shoulder and fallen fast asleep.

When Amanda began to stir early in the morning, Henriette had smoothed her hair and straightened her clothes as best she could. She was eager to make a good impression on her new mistress, although deep in her heart she knew that her appearance would not really make a difference. The bond between a doll and the child she belongs to is very strong. Henriette knew that she would love Amanda no matter what Amanda looked like, and she was quite sure that Amanda would feel the same. Nevertheless, Henriette was a doll who took special pride in her appearance. These mud spatters on her dress simply had to go.

Henriette looked around and spied a glass of water on the nightstand next to the bed. She got up and tiptoed over to it. Henriette reached out to dip her handkerchief into the water, but the glass was too tall. She couldn't quite reach it from the bed. Now another doll might have been discouraged, but not Henriette. She picked up her skirt and stepped gracefully over onto the nightstand. From there it was easy to wet her handkerchief.

She was just beginning to rub at one of the

worst spots on the hem of her gown when she heard someone say, "You-all might as well give it up, honey. That dress won't ever come clean."

Henriette dropped her handkerchief and whirled around. As she turned, her enormous hoopskirt swept against the side of the glass and knocked it over. Water splashed everywhere. Henriette reached out to catch the glass, but it spun away and crashed to the floor, breaking into a hundred pieces. Suddenly Henriette lost her footing and sat down hard in the puddle of water.

This amazing series of events was accompanied by a chorus of small voices shouting,

"Look out," and "Watch the glass," followed by complete silence. Henriette sat in the puddle with water dripping off her nose. Finally the voice that had startled Henriette in the first place said, "I'm sorry, honey. I didn't mean to scare you."

Henriette wiped a drop of water off her nose and turned to see where the voice had come from.

Over in the corner of the room was a battered toy box. Ragtag dolls and stuffed animals were spilling out of the box onto the floor. They were a sorry-looking lot, but at the moment their faces seemed to be filled with genuine concern for Henriette's predicament.

The doll that spoke was a big cloth doll. Her face was a kind of grimy gray. Her head was covered with tufts of faded orange yarn. She was stuffed with corn husks, which gave her a tough, spiky appearance. But her voice, with its slow southern drawl, had a friendly sound to it.

"Did you-all hurt yourself, honey?"

"Oh, no. I am quite all right," said Henriette as she stood up and began to wring water out of the hem of her skirt. "It is just that I am not certain what to do about all this mess."

"Pardon me, madam. Perhaps I can be of assistance." A rather old and battered toy soldier stuck his head up out of the toy box. "Colonel Rusticuffs at your service."

"*Bonjour, monsieur*," said Henriette, slipping once again into her native language.

"I hate to see a lady in distress," said Colonel Rusticuffs. "If you will allow me, I'd be happy to organize a ground detail to take care of the broken glass."

"Oh, yes, please," replied Henriette. "I would be most grateful for your assistance."

"Very well," said the Colonel. "Troops, fall

in." One by one the dolls and toys tumbled out of the toy box. There was a baby doll in a pink pinafore and a rag doll in a calico dress. They were followed by a corncob doll and a wooden horse with a broken tail. There were three tin soldiers, a clown with a red nose, and an assortment of cloth animals, including a stuffed rabbit with floppy ears, a brown bear, and a spotted pig with a bell around his neck.

The Colonel, who walked with a limp, told the dolls to form a line between "the disaster area" and the wastebasket. One by one they picked up the pieces of broken glass, being very careful not to cut their fingers or paws, and passed them down along the line. The tallest dolls at the end of the line threw the pieces of broken glass into the wastebasket and the baby doll swept up the splinters with a whisk broom.

Henriette, who was stranded on the top of the nightstand, watched with great admiration.

Chapter Three

THE job was done quickly. Colonel Rusticuffs thanked his troops and marched them back to the toy box. The big doll with the orange hair came over and climbed up on Amanda's bed. "Now, honey. Let's see what we can do about the mess up here."

"I am so sorry for all of this," said Henriette. "You must think I am quite a bother."

"Don't you say another word," said the big doll. "It's all my fault. I shouldn't have spoken up so sudden. My name's Ginger."

"*Bonjour*, Ginger. My name is Henriette. I am very happy to meet you."

"The pleasure's all mine," said Ginger. "But listen, Henriette, what we need is a hanky or two. I think there might be some in this here drawer. See if you can't grab that knob over there."

Without wasting a moment, Henriette pushed her heavy wet skirt out of the way, got down on her stomach and reached out over the edge of the nightstand. She grabbed the knob on the left while Ginger grabbed the knob on the right. They both pulled together and the drawer slid open.

"Now, you-all toss me one of them hankies," said Ginger, "and we'll have the place dry as a bone in no time at all."

Henriette pulled one handkerchief out of the drawer and gave it to Ginger. She took another herself and began mopping up the water. As they worked Ginger said, "I saw you come in late last night. Looked like you was all tired out."

"Yes, I must confess I was exhausted."

"That little girl Amanda . . . is she someone special to you?" asked Ginger.

"Oh, yes! Amanda is very special to me. She is my rightful mistress. Since I came from France, I have been passed down through three generations of little girls in her family. Her grandmother, Mrs. Amanda Wellington Cartwright, was my first mistress. After that I belonged to her mother, and now I belong to Amanda."

"What happened to Amanda's folks?" asked Ginger.

"The family was separated during the war. I stayed with Amanda's grandmother, so there is much that is unclear to me." Henriette stopped mopping for a moment and leaned against the candlestick to rest. "Amanda's father was a soldier," she went on. "It is my belief that he was killed in the fighting. After the war my old mistress found Amanda's mother's grave, but she could not find Amanda. She spent years searching for her granddaughter. Finally a child was located at this orphanage."

"How did Mrs. Cartwright know that Amanda was her granddaughter?"

"The woman who runs the orphanage, Mrs.

Crabtree, sent Amanda's locket along as identification. My old mistress recognized it at once. It had belonged to Amanda's mother."

Ginger stopped mopping for a moment. She sat back on her heels and said to Henriette, "I don't get it. If the grandmother knew about Amanda, why didn't she send for her?"

"Amanda's grandmother is a very old woman and not in good health. She decided that Amanda would be better off in the orphanage, where some young family might adopt her."

"It must have been hard for you to leave your old mistress," said Ginger.

"Oh, yes, it was a very difficult decision to make. But in the end I knew — a doll's place is with the *child* she belongs to." Henriette picked up her handkerchief and went back to work.

"Gee, it must be nice to belong to someone," said Ginger. "I been knockin' around so long by myself I don't even remember what it's like anymore, havin' a little girl of my own."

"What about all the children here?" asked Henriette.

Ginger sighed.

"Well, they play with us sometimes. But it's like this, Henriette, we're all orphans here. . . . Charity cases . . . nobody belongs to anybody. . . ."

"But this is not good," said Henriette.

"That's a fact," said Ginger.

Henriette and Ginger worked well together. Soon there wasn't a trace of water left on the nightstand. "Well," said Ginger. "I better be gettin' back to the toy box. Breakfast will be over in no time. We wouldn't want the girls to catch us up to no good."

"Thank you, Ginger," said Henriette. "I hope that I can repay the kindness some day."

"Maybe you-all can teach me some of them nice manners you got," said Ginger.

"It would be a pleasure," said Henriette.

"See you-all later!" said Ginger as she climbed down off Amanda's bed.

"*Au revoir*, my friend. Good-bye," said Henriette. And then she thought to herself, what good luck to meet so many new friends on my first day here!

Chapter Four

AMANDA found Henriette sitting on the nightstand next to her bed when she came back from breakfast. This seemed odd but not as odd as the fact that Henriette's gown was soaking wet. Amanda couldn't imagine how this could have happened. She began to look around for clues, but almost at once her curiosity gave way to motherly concern.

Amanda had never owned a doll as elegant and fragile as this one, and yet she knew just how to take care of her. Carefully she picked up Henriette and placed her on the bed. She unfastened the hooks at the back of Henriette's gown, and very gently pulled the dress up over her head.

The blue satin gown was covered with hand-painted pink forget-me-nots. The neck, cut very low, was edged with lace. The sleeves were puffed, and the giant hoopskirt fell to the floor in three flounces. Even though it was torn in two places and covered with mud, anyone could see that it was a dress fit for a tiny princess.

Amanda removed Henriette's hoopskirt, petticoats, and corset, all of which were a little damp, and put them on the windowsill to dry. She took off the one remaining shoe, wondering what had become of the other, and put it away in the drawer. Then she wrapped Henriette in a fluffy white towel and put her to bed.

Amanda tucked the covers up under Henriette's chin, kissed her on the forehead, and told her she must try to get some rest. Henriette lay on the soft pillow, thinking how safe and happy she felt, and drifted off to sleep.

While Henriette slept, Amanda washed and mended the lovely sky-blue gown. She scrubbed the mud spots on the skirt until it was so clean you could almost smell the hand-painted pink forget-me-nots. The dress would never look like new again, but Amanda thought it was the most beautiful gown she had ever seen.

Henriette stayed tucked in bed all day, while Amanda told her stories to pass the time. Henriette learned a great deal about her little mistress that rainy afternoon, and she loved her more as every moment passed.

The other little girls came and went throughout the day, but Henriette and Amanda paid no attention to them. They were safe and cozy in their own little world. Occasionally Henriette dozed off to sleep, but each time she awoke, Amanda was there, sitting quietly by her side, just as Henriette had always imagined it would be.

Chapter Five

Bright and early the next morning the housemaid, Nellie, told Amanda she was wanted down in Mrs. Crabtree's office. Everyone in the orphanage was talking about Amanda's new doll. Naturally, Mrs. Crabtree had some questions to ask.

When Amanda went downstairs she took Henriette along. By this time Henriette's clothing was clean and dry. Amanda had combed her honey-colored curls, and except for her bare feet, Henriette looked very presentable.

Amanda held on tightly to Henriette as she walked down the huge curving staircase. She had a solemn expression on her pretty face, like a soldier approaching a firing squad. You see, Amanda was afraid of Mrs. Crabtree. It's not that Mrs. Crabtree was a bad person. There were just too many little girls, and not enough time, space, or money to look after all of them properly. As a result Mrs. Crabtree seldom smiled and often seemed angry.

At the foot of the staircase Amanda turned right and walked down a long hallway. She stopped outside the office to straighten Henriette's dress, then knocked timidly on the door.

"Come in," said Mrs. Crabtree.

Amanda opened the door. Mrs. Crabtree was sitting at her desk, writing a letter. "Come in and sit down Amanda, I'll be with you presently."

"Yes, ma'am," said Amanda quietly. She crossed the room and sat down on a hard wooden chair across the desk from Mrs. Crabtree.

After a moment Mrs. Crabtree put down her fountain pen, and picked up her eyeglasses. She polished them with her handkerchief, then put them on and took a long look at

Henriette. Henriette felt very uncomfortable. She thought it very bad manners of Mrs. Crabtree to stare at her in that way.

Finally Mrs. Crabtree said, "I see you have a new doll, Amanda."

"Yes, ma'am," said Amanda.

"Did you find her out in the school yard?" asked Mrs. Crabtree.

"No, ma'am," said Amanda.

"Or perhaps, on the way back from church last Sunday?"

"No, ma'am," said Amanda. "I found her at the foot of my bed."

"At the foot of your bed! Do you have any idea how she got there?" asked Mrs. Crabtree.

"No," said Amanda. "But I know that I belong to her and she belongs to me."

"Oh, really?" said Mrs. Crabtree. "And how do you know that?"

"I'm not sure," said Amanda. "But I know that it's true, just as I know that her name is Henriette, and look . . . she brought me back my locket."

Mrs. Crabtree stared at the shiny gold locket hanging around Amanda's neck for some moments, then took off her glasses and pinched the bridge of her nose. Mrs. Crabtree often did this when she was at a loss for words. After a moment Mrs. Crabtree looked directly at Amanda and said, "All right, young lady. You may keep the doll. At least until someone claims her. Now run along, I have work to do."

Amanda got down off the chair and ran out of the room before Mrs. Crabtree had a chance to change her mind.

When Amanda was gone, Mrs. Crabtree got up and locked the door. She paced back and forth several times across the floor, then sat down at her desk to think. Something very strange was going on. She distinctly remembered sending Amanda's locket to a woman named Mrs. Amanda Wellington Cartwright, who lived on a plantation all the way across the state of Georgia, and who believed Amanda to be her long-lost granddaughter. How had the child come to have the locket again? And what about this doll?

Mrs. Crabtree began drumming her fingers on the top of her desk. This business was a mystery, and Mrs. Crabtree was not a woman who enjoyed mysteries until they were solved.

Finally, after a good deal of thought, Mrs. Crabtree pulled out a sheet of paper, took up her pen, and wrote a short note to Mrs. Cartwright. She explained that Amanda's locket had apparently been returned, and that somehow Amanda had acquired a rather distinguished-looking china doll.

Mrs. Crabtree thought these items must have been sent by post from Mrs. Cartwright. She noted that the orphanage was grateful for assistance, but that, in the future, to avoid confusion, all gifts should be sent through her.

Chapter Six

IN the days that followed, Henriette and Amanda became the best of friends. Amanda played with Henriette all day long, and at night took her to bed. At first Henriette was concerned because her little dark-haired mistress seemed so sad and serious.

She sometimes wished she could talk with Amanda the way she did with Ginger. But that is not the way with dolls and children. It's not that dolls never speak to children. They sometimes do, but only when it's very important. Their voices have a melody and pitch that only children can hear. Henriette knew she could speak to Amanda if it was absolutely necessary — just as she had on the first morning they met.

In the evenings after Amanda had gone to sleep, Henriette often climbed out of bed and went to visit her friends in the toy box. Henriette came to know them all by name: the baby doll, Celeste; and Willa, the rag doll with the calico dress; and Maisie, the corn-husk doll. Henriette liked them all, but Ginger became her special friend.

One day several weeks after Henriette had come to the orphanage, Amanda was playing quietly in the dormitory. All the other girls were outside. Mrs. Crabtree came into the room, carrying a large box. It was wrapped in brown paper and tied up with string.

"Amanda," said Mrs. Crabtree. "I have something for you."

"For me?" said Amanda.

Mrs. Crabtree placed the package on the bed next to Amanda. "Why don't you open it?" she said.

Amanda put Henriette carefully aside and began to unwrap the package. She untied the string, tore away the paper, and opened the box.

Inside was a miniature steamer trunk with leather handles and a brass lock. As soon as Henriette saw the trunk, her heart took a tiny leap. It was an old and familiar sight to her. For as long as Henriette could remember, this trunk sat under the curio cabinet in her old mistress's drawing room.

Amanda lifted the lid of the trunk and looked inside. It was filled to the brim with the extensive wardrobe of a medium-sized china doll. There were morning dresses, tea frocks, and evening gowns in every color of the rainbow, along with bonnets and gloves for every occasion. There was an entire row of tiny satin slippers to match every outfit, and all of it, of course, belonged to Henriette.

Inside the trunk, on top of the doll clothes, was a small white envelope. It was addressed to Amanda. Amanda picked up the envelope and turned it over in her hands.

"Shall I read it to you, Amanda?" said Mrs. Crabtree.

"Yes, please," answered Amanda.

Mrs. Crabtree opened the envelope and took out one sheet of paper. The letter inside was written by hand. It read:

My dear Amanda,

You have already received the first part of your rightful inheritance from me . . . and here, safe inside Henriette's trunk, is the rest.

Your loving grandmother,

Amanda Wellington Cartwright

P.S. Tell my oldest friend, Henriette, that I have placed your future in her hands.

"My grandmother?" said Amanda with a puzzled expression on her face. "I didn't know I had a grandmother."

"Yes. Well . . ." said Mrs. Crabtree. "This woman, Mrs. Cartwright, apparently believes you are her granddaughter, although she has not produced any real evidence to prove it."

"But she must be my grandmother," said Amanda, "because she knows all about Henriette!"

"Be that as it may . . ." began Mrs. Crabtree, but Amanda, in her growing excitement, forgot her manners and interrupted her.

"Where does my grandmother live?" asked Amanda.

"She lives a great distance from here. And I must tell you, Amanda," said Mrs. Crabtree finally coming to the point, "that Mrs. Cartwright is a very old woman, and in very poor health. She wrote to me some weeks ago, explaining the situation. So you must not get your hopes up. Your future is here with us."

"Oh, I see," said Amanda.

"However," said Mrs. Crabtree. "We must write to Mrs. Cartwright immediately and thank her for the lovely gift."

Amanda went off with Mrs. Crabtree, leaving Henriette alone in the dormitory. As soon as they were gone, Henriette tiptoed across the bed and picked up the note. She smiled when she recognized her old mistress's handwriting, but then a frown passed across her face.

"What can be the meaning of this puzzling note?" said Henriette to herself. "Surely my wardrobe is not the sum of Amanda's inheritance from her grandmother. What about the plantation? What about the beautiful old house that I grew up in? And what on earth could be the meaning of this mysterious postscript?"

Henriette shook her head and wondered if she would ever be able to figure it out.

Chapter Seven

AFTER Amanda finished her letter she returned to the dormitory. It was almost lunchtime. Most of the children had come in from the yard. Amanda began taking the beautiful doll dresses out of the trunk and holding them up for everyone to see.

Each dress was lovelier than the one before. All the girls were admiring the dresses except for Rachel, who stood off to one side with a sulky expression on her face.

Every detail of every costume was perfect, from the tiny pearl buttons on the sleeves to the ostrich feathers on the hats. There were so many lovely things that Amanda couldn't decide what to put on Henriette first.

She picked up each gown and put it down again, then finally decided on a dove-gray afternoon dress with an overskirt of deep turquoise. It had white eyelet lace at the collar and cuffs, and suited Henriette's complexion perfectly. Amanda put a pair of black patent-leather slippers on Henriette's tiny feet, and tied a hand-embroidered oriental shawl around her shoulders.

"She looks beautiful," said Molly.

All the other girls agreed except Rachel, who made a face and said, "You make me sick. All this fuss over a bunch of old doll dresses!"

Suddenly Rachel picked up one of the dresses Amanda had taken out of the trunk and threw it on the floor.

"Don't do that," said Amanda. But Rachel paid no attention.

"And this dumb doll you treat like a queen. The next thing you know, we'll all have to bow before we come into the room!"

Rachel was getting angrier and angrier. She

began taking all the dresses out of the trunk and throwing them on the floor.

"Rachel, stop it!" cried Amanda. But it didn't do any good. Rachel tore a feather off one of the hats and ripped a piece of lace off a pair of pantaloons. Some of the smaller girls were frightened and backed away.

Amanda tried to push Rachel away, but Rachel was bigger and stronger, and wouldn't budge.

"If you don't stop right now," said Amanda. "I'm going to go tell Mrs. Crabtree!"

"Go ahead, tell her," sneered Rachel. "See if I care, tattletale!"

Not knowing what else she could do, Amanda ran out of the room and down the big staircase to Mrs. Crabtree's office.

During all of this, Henriette didn't move a muscle. She sat on the pillow and didn't so much as blink her eye. She was angry with herself. She should have known that Rachel would cause trouble sooner or later. Perhaps she could have prevented it. At the moment she could only hope to ride out the storm.

Just then Rachel turned to Henriette and said, "This will fix Amanda!" She grabbed Henriette roughly by the waist and ran out of the room.

At the end of the upstairs hallway was a small door. It looked like a cupboard door, but it was low and close to the floor. Rachel was heading straight toward it. When she got to the end of the hall, Rachel opened the little door and hurled Henriette, head over heels, down the laundry chute.

Chapter Eight

IT all happened so fast that Henriette didn't
really have time to be frightened. In a flurry
of flying petticoats, she went tumbling down
the long chute that led to the cellar. Down,
down, down into the darkness she fell. Henriette landed with a thump in a basket of dirty
sheets and towels.

Even after she hit bottom, it took Henriette
a moment to realize what had happened. She
sat up in the basket and blinked several times,
trying to get her bearings.

She looked around the cellar at the wash
tubs and scrub boards, then leaned back and
looked up the dark chute through which she
had fallen. Suddenly her little heart began to

race and she started to tremble all over. It was hard not to imagine what would have happened if the basket at the bottom of the chute had been empty. Henriette was not at all a cowardly doll, but every now and then even the bravest of dolls gets frightened.

Suddenly Henriette began to count backward in French. She often did this when she was frightened. She started at ninety-nine.

"Quatre-vingt-dix-neuf, quatre-vingt-dix-huit, quatre-vingt-dix-sept. . . ."

By the time she got to seventy-three, Henriette was feeling much better. She stood up, straightened her dress, and smoothed her hair. It was all very well to find oneself safe and in one piece after a long fall, but now Henriette had to find a way out of the cellar.

She climbed out of the basket and began looking around. Everything was covered with dust and cobwebs. The cellar had a dirt floor so Henriette held up her skirts as she walked.

She made her way carefully around to the other side of the washtubs and found the cellar stairs. But even from the bottom Henriette could see that the door at the top of the stairs was tightly closed. There were several windows in the cellar, but they were all up high near to the ceiling, and none of them seemed to be open. Henriette was trapped. She sat down on a small overturned pail and said to herself, "I suppose I shall simply have to wait until Amanda comes to rescue me."

It was just about then that she heard a sound, a quiet rumbling, almost like faraway thunder. After a moment Henriette realized it was the sound of a cat purring. She looked up and saw a calico cat sitting on top of the washtub.

At first Henriette was alarmed, but then she smiled and breathed a sigh of relief. Ordinarily she was not at all comfortable in the company of animals, but this cat was different. She was, in a way, a friend. Henriette had met the cat the night she arrived at the orphanage. The front door had been locked up tight, leaving Henriette wondering what to do next. Suddenly the cat had appeared and led her to a secret entrance, a door just big enough for a cat — and a doll — to enter.

"*Bonjour, mademoiselle,*" Henriette said to her calico friend. "How are you today?"

Of course, the cat didn't answer; Henriette

didn't expect her to. Even dolls know that cats don't talk.

The cat didn't seem to be very interested in Henriette this time. She blinked, then turned her attention to a mouse that was scurrying across the cellar floor. Henriette watched the cat watch the mouse for some time, but after a while her thoughts turned back to her own situation.

"Pardon me, *mademoiselle*," said Henriette to the cat. "Could you possibly show me a way out of here?"

It was just about then that the cat pounced. She had been watching and waiting for the perfect opportunity and now it had come. She leapt from the top of the washtub and landed gracefully right on target. But the mouse was too fast. It dashed into a hole at the foot of the stairs.

"Now if I were as small as a mouse," said Henriette to herself, "I could dash into a mouse hole and I'm sure I would find my way in no time. But, alas, I am a doll, and there is no magic tunnel for me."

The cat crouched next to the washtub and waited for the mouse. A moment passed, then two or three. After a time the cat seemed to lose interest. She yawned and stretched, then walked off across the cellar floor. When she got to the door, she turned and gave Henriette the strangest look. Out of curiosity Henriette decided to follow. The cat was moving slowly, but Henriette had to run to catch up.

When they got to the other side of the cellar, Henriette realized that they were in a scullery, a kind of second kitchen that wasn't often used. The cat circled the foot of the stove once or twice, then jumped up on top of it. From there she made another graceful leap to the top of a cart that was standing against a column.

Henriette noticed that it wasn't really a column, it was a shaft with a door in it. The door was open and showed a small closed chamber. The cat walked into the chamber, turned her back on Henriette, and curled up elegantly in the corner. Henriette was just about to say something to the cat when suddenly the door of the chamber closed. Immediately after that a bell rang, and there was a loud squeaking sound that startled Henriette. Henriette jumped, then dashed behind a shovel to hide.

The squeaking noise went on for some time — then stopped, and then began again. Henriette put her fingers in her ears. When the noise finally stopped again, Henriette peeped around the side of the shovel. She saw the door of the compartment slide open. But, much to her amazement, the cat was gone.

Chapter Nine

Henriette was just beginning to recover from the surprise of the disappearing cat when suddenly she heard keys rattling at the cellar door.

"*Tiens!*" said Henriette out loud. "The rescue party is on the way, and where am I? Wandering off never to be found again!" Henriette picked up her skirts and ran as fast as she could back to the laundry room.

She managed to climb back into the laundry basket just as Mrs. Crabtree reached the foot of the stairs. Amanda and Rachel followed close behind. Henriette noticed that Mrs. Crabtree was carrying the wardrobe trunk, and wondered why.

"Now let me see," said Mrs. Crabtree. "If I'm not mistaken, the laundry chute empties out right about here. . . . You see, Amanda, there's your doll."

As soon as Amanda saw Henriette, she ran over to the laundry basket and knelt down beside it. She picked Henriette up very gently, making sure that nothing was broken, then hugged her and whispered, "Oh, Henriette. I was so worried. I was afraid I would never see you again."

"Now, Rachel," said Mrs. Crabtree. "You must apologize to Amanda. It was very bad of you to throw her doll down the laundry chute."

"I'm sorry," said Rachel. "I won't do it again." But Henriette could see that Rachel wasn't sorry in the least.

"Now, Amanda," said Mrs. Crabtree. "We've had just about enough nonsense over this doll. To avoid further trouble I think we'll just put this trunk away for the time being."

"But. . ." said Amanda.

"No buts about it," said Mrs. Crabtree. "I won't have any more of this kind of behavior.

The trunk and all these fancy dresses will be perfectly safe down here in the cellar."

Mrs. Crabtree put the little steamer trunk in the corner next to a stack of boxes and suitcases. Amanda didn't say anything. She was trying very hard not to cry.

"Now come along, girls," said Mrs. Crabtree. "It's time for lessons."

Amanda followed Mrs. Crabtree out of the cellar. Rachel, who hadn't said a word, brought up the rear with a smug expression on her face.

Chapter Ten

AFTER the incident with the laundry chute, Rachel seemed to lose interest in teasing Amanda. Henriette was very grateful. She spent the long afternoons with Amanda and in the evening after the children had gone to sleep, Henriette held etiquette classes for some of the dolls that lived in the toy box.

She taught the dolls manners and deportment. She gave them exercises to develop grace and proper carriage, as well as lessons to improve their speech and grammar. Ginger was her star pupil.

Henriette even taught them to dance. For this she enlisted the services of Colonel Rusticuffs. The Colonel protested that he was too old and rusty to dance. But in truth, he could waltz with the best of them.

One day the dolls found a rather chipped but usable tea set at the bottom of the toy box. Henriette decided to give a tea party.

All the dolls were invited. However, on the evening of the tea party, Henriette was told by Maisie, the corncob doll, that Ginger wasn't coming. Henriette was very surprised and went to look for Ginger. She found her sitting on the floor behind the toy box, looking forlorn.

"Ginger," said Henriette. "Why aren't you coming to my tea party?"

"I don't have anything nice to wear," said Ginger with a sigh.

"But this is of no importance," said Henriette. "You look lovely just the way you are."

"No, I don't," said Ginger. "Why bother having good manners if you look awful?"

"To me, you do not look awful. You look tall and brave and very strong," said Henriette.

"No, I look awful. Rachel said so."

"But, my friend, *mon amie*," exclaimed Henriette. "You must not listen to Rachel. She is a very unhappy child with nothing but jealousy in her heart."

"I know that," said Ginger. "But maybe if I had nice clothes like you got then I'd have a little girl to belong to."

"Someday, Ginger, a little girl will take you for her very own and she will love you dearly. But not because you have pretty clothes."

"Do you really think so?" asked Ginger hopefully.

"I am certain of it," said Henriette. "But in the meantime, just to cheer you up, why don't you take my shawl."

"No, I couldn't," said Ginger.

"Why not?" asked Henriette. "It is mine to give and I would love for you to have it."

With no more buts about it Henriette tied the lovely oriental shawl around Ginger's shoulders and kissed her lightly on both cheeks.

"Now, come along, Ginger. It's teatime."

Henriette arranged toy blocks in a circle for the dolls to sit on. She laid out the tea service on a small box, and used one of Amanda's handkerchiefs as a table cloth. Colonel Rusticuffs and the three tin soldiers showed the ladies to their seats.

The dolls all looked their very best. Celeste had washed her face and pressed her pinafore and Willa was wearing a new red bandanna. The corncob doll sat stiffly in her chair and the three tin soldiers were as nervous as new cadets.

Henriette, with the Colonel on her right, poured the tea. Ginger served the tea cakes. Henriette taught the dolls how to place their

napkins, and how to hold a teacup with the pinky finger up. This was very difficult for the rag dolls, because their hands were shaped like mittens, but they managed somehow. Henriette pointed out that speaking with your mouth full was frowned upon, and that generally a well-bred doll didn't drink out of his or her saucer. Of course, the teacups were empty and so were the cake plates. Dolls don't really eat, but it was fun to pretend.

When the party began to draw to a close Ginger said, "Well, that was fun. Now there's nothing left but the washing up."

"Oh, my!" said Celeste. "Do we have to wash the dishes?"

"No, of course not," said Ginger. "We'll just send 'em down to the kitchen in the dumbwaiter."

"What is a dumbwaiter?" asked Henriette.

"It's a small elevator the cook uses to carry food and dishes from the kitchen to the floors above."

"A dumbwaiter!" said Henriette. "Of course! That's what it was. The cat disappeared into the dumbwaiter!"

"What's that, Henriette?" asked Ginger.

"The day I fell down the laundry chute I saw a calico cat climb into the dumbwaiter and disappear. At the time I didn't know what it was!"

"Henriette, honey," said Ginger. "You're too polite. You-all didn't fall down the laundry chute. That rotten Rachel threw you down the laundry chute!"

"We were talking about the dumbwaiter," said Henriette. "How does it work?"

"I believe I can explain," said the Colonel. "The elevator compartment is moved up and down by a set of ropes and pulleys. A very simple system. I should think even a doll could work it."

"A doll all by herself?" said Henriette.

"Well, perhaps it would take several dolls," said the Colonel. "But, of course, we all know there is no end to what a really determined doll can do."

"Here, here," said Ginger raising her teacup. "I'll drink to that!"

After the tea party ended, Ginger caught hold of Henriette's elbow and whispered, "Why did you-all ask them questions about the dumb-waiter?"

"I'm not sure," said Henriette.

"Just don't get any funny ideas, honey. Them things can be dangerous."

"Yes, I'm sure you are correct, Ginger," said Henriette. "Thank you for your concern. Good-night, sleep well."

Henriette crawled back into bed with Amanda. When she fell asleep, she had a dream. In the dream she was riding in the dumbwaiter, and Ginger was with her. It was a very exciting dream. But in the morning she had forgotten all about it.

Chapter Eleven

THE day after the tea party, Mrs. Crabtree sent for Amanda. Amanda picked up Henriette and started down the stairs. When she got to the office door, Mrs. Crabtree was waiting for her.

"Come in, Amanda," said Mrs. Crabtree. "I've been waiting for you."

Amanda sat down on the hard wooden chair and put Henriette on the corner of the desk.

"I have some unhappy news to tell you, Amanda. I have just received word that Mrs. Amanda Wellington Cartwright, the woman who claimed to have been your grandmother, has passed away. Apparently no will has been found, nor any other legal document establishing your relationship to her. I realize that you did not personally know Mrs. Cartwright, but I thought you should be told."

"Thank you for telling me," said Amanda in a voice so small that Henriette could hardly hear her.

"Here is a copy of the letter I have received." Mrs. Crabtree took the letter out of a drawer and put it on the desk in front of Amanda. Amanda just sat there. She seemed confused and a little lost.

"I'll give you a moment by yourself, Amanda. When you're ready, you may run along to supper.

Mrs. Crabtree left the room and closed the door behind her. Amanda picked up Henriette and held her tightly in her arms. The doll looked at the letter lying on the desk. It was from the law firm of Jacob and Wilder. It began:

To Mrs. Rebecca Crabtree,
City Orphanage, Atlanta, Georgia:

We understand that you have been corresponding with Mrs. Amanda Wellington Cartwright concerning an orphan in your care. We regret to inform you. . .

Suddenly Henriette's eyes began to blur. Mrs. Amanda Wellington Cartwright had been Henriette's first mistress and her oldest friend. She would miss her greatly.

As the afternoon light began to fade Henriette looked up at Amanda and thought to herself, poor little girl. She really is an orphan now.

Chapter Twelve

IF Henriette thought Amanda's troubles with Rachel were over, she was mistaken. One afternoon two weeks later it began all over again. Amanda was sitting on the floor near the toy box with Molly and Emily. Henriette was sitting comfortably on Amanda's lap. Ginger and the rest of the dolls were hanging over the sides of the toy box.

Amanda was telling Molly and Emily about her locket. She took it off to show it to them. Very carefully she opened it so they could see the pictures inside.

"This is a picture of me when I was very small," said Amanda with a very solemn expression on her face. "And this is my father."

Just then Rachel, who had been lying on her bed, said, "How do you know it's your father?"

"I just know it is," said Amanda.

Rachel got off her bed and started walking toward Amanda.

"Let me see that picture," said Rachel.

"No," said Amanda. She stood up and began to back away.

"Let me see that picture, or I'll take your doll away from you again."

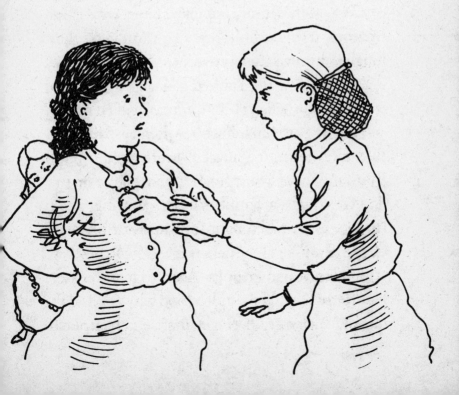

"No," said Amanda, holding Henriette behind her back.

"Show her the picture," said Molly.

"You better show it to me," said Rachel.

"All right," said Amanda. "You can look at it, but you can't touch it."

Amanda held the locket out at arm's length. Rachel took one look at the picture and said, "He's wearing a uniform."

"My papa was a soldier," said Amanda. "He fought in the war and died for the South!"

"Oh, yeah?" said Rachel. "Then why is he wearing a blue uniform? The soldiers that fought on our side wore gray. Your father was a Yankee. A dirty Yankee traitor."

Rachel turned on her heel and walked away.

That night Amanda cried herself to sleep. But Henriette lay awake for a long time, thinking about what Rachel had said. Amanda's father was a Yankee. In the War Between the States he had fought for the North instead of the South.

Suddenly many things began to make sense. Henriette had never understood why Amanda's mother had run off to get married. Henriette knew that she had married a soldier. She had always assumed that he was a soldier in the southern army. After the wedding Sarah never came home to visit, and the family never talked about her husband. The only thing Henriette knew about him was his name — Jonathan Edward Conkey.

A thought struck Henriette like a bolt of lightning. What if Amanda had relatives on her father's side — relatives in the North that Amanda's grandmother had never tried to contact? That very moment Henriette decided she would do everything in her power to find out. If Amanda had relatives, they might want to adopt her, and Amanda would have a home at last.

Chapter Thirteen

As soon as all the children were asleep and the house was quiet, Henriette got out of bed. She tiptoed out of the dormitory and headed toward the great winding staircase. She considered sliding down the banister, but there was always the danger of falling off at the end. She would have to go down on foot.

Climbing down one stair after another, it took Henriette nearly half an hour to reach the first floor.

When she finally got to the foot of the stairs, she tiptoed down the hallway toward Mrs. Crabtree's office. She had fingers crossed on both hands, hoping and praying that she would find the door unlocked.

Luckily it was! When she got to the office, she gave the door a mighty shove and it swung open. Henriette slipped in and ran across the room to the desk.

She climbed up on the chair and from there stepped over onto the desk. It was covered with books and ledgers, along with stacks of letters and documents. On the far side of the desk was an inkwell, a paperweight with a rose in it, and a slingshot, no doubt taken away from one of the children. Henriette took a piece of writing paper out of the drawer and was just beginning to look around for a pen when she noticed something on the desk that had not been there before. It was a brand-new shiny black typewriter. Henriette had never seen a typewriter before, except in magazine pictures. The small black machine with large round keys looked fascinating to Henriette.

"I wonder how difficult it would be for a medium-sized china doll to use a typewriter? I suppose there is only one way to find out."

Henriette walked across the desk, dragging the large piece of paper behind her. She managed with some difficulty to get the paper into the roller. Turning the roller was another

matter. To Henriette, the handle on the roller looked like a giant factory wheel.

But she was not easily discouraged. Henriette pushed up her sleeves, and put a little spit on her palms, then grabbed the wheel with both hands and began to turn. Little by little the paper fed into the machine.

When that was done Henriette walked around the typewriter and stood in front of the keyboard.

" 'To whom it may concern'. . . . now let me see," said Henriette. "Where is the 'T'? Ah, there it is, right next to the 'R.' "

Henriette put both hands on the key and pressed down with all her might. A lovely black T appeared on the paper. Henriette was delighted. "You see, there is nothing to it. What a marvelous invention!" she said to herself.

It took Henriette the better part of the night to complete a letter to the War Department in Washington, D.C. When it was finished, she took it out of the typewriter. Kneeling down on the paper, and holding the pen with both hands, Henriette managed to sign Mrs. Crabtree's name. The letter was written on behalf of an orphan named Amanda Conkey requesting information on next of kin to Jonathan Edward Conkey.

When the letter was safely buried at the bottom of a pile of letters in the outgoing mail basket, Henriette began the long, weary climb up the stairs. Dawn was breaking as Henriette finally crawled back into bed and fell asleep with her head on Amanda's shoulder.

Chapter Fourteen

Henriette managed to sneak away at least once a week just about the time the mail was to be delivered. She would hide under the hall table and wait until the letters came flying through the slot in the door. As soon as they hit the floor Henriette would dash out from her hiding place and look through them as quickly as possible. To her great disappointment, Henriette never saw any letters from the War Department.

Once or twice in the middle of the night Henriette made the long trip down to Mrs. Crabtree's office. She searched the desk and the drawers but never found what she was looking for.

Henriette was often troubled when she thought about her first mistress. She couldn't believe that Mrs. Cartwright had not left a will naming Amanda as her heir. These thoughts always led Henriette back to the puzzling note that had come with her wardrobe. *Tell my oldest friend, Henriette, that I have placed your future in her hands.* Henriette had recalled the words a thousand times, but still could not guess what her old mistress was trying to say.

One day almost two months later, Amanda and Henriette were outside playing under a tree in the yard. Molly came running up to them. She said that Amanda was to go inside, put on a clean dress, and go down to Mrs. Crabtree's office.

Amanda had no idea what the fuss was all about. But Henriette had the feeling that something wonderful was about to happen. Amanda hurried inside, washed her face, and went down to Mrs. Crabtree's office. When Amanda walked through the door, Henriette was safely tucked into the crook of her arm.

Mrs. Crabtree was sitting at her desk. There were two other people in the room. One was a distinguished-looking gentleman, holding a stovepipe hat in his hand. The other was a beautiful young woman in a lavender traveling suit. Something about the woman looked familiar to Henriette.

"Amanda," said Mrs. Crabtree. "Come in and close the door." Then turning to the couple she said, "I believe this is the child you asked about. Amanda, say hello to Mr. and Mrs. Steven Forsythe."

"How do you do," said Amanda very quietly.

"Oh, Steven," said the young woman to her husband, "she has Jonathan's eyes."

"Now, now, Evelyn. Let's not jump to conclusions," said Mr. Forsythe. Then turning to Mrs. Crabtree he said, "You see, we received a letter from the War Department in Washington informing us about your request."

"What request?" asked Mrs. Crabtree.

"For information regarding next of kin to Jonathan Edward Conkey."

"I wrote no such letter," said Mrs. Crabtree.

"But surely . . . well, never mind. The

child's name is Amanda Conkey, is it not?"
asked Mr. Forsythe.

"The child's name is Amanda, as to Conkey
that's hard to say. There was a woman named
Amanda Wellington Cartwright who believed
this child to be her granddaughter. Unfortu-
nately, Mrs. Cartwright passed away. The
child's identity has never been established."

"You see," Mr. Forsythe turned to his wife.
"I told you this would be a wild goose chase."

"But Steven," said the lady in the lavender
dress. "She's such a lovely child, and I swear
she looks just like my brother."

Henriette's heart began to beat very fast.
This was the answer to her prayers. Amanda
had a family after all.

Mr. Forsythe did not seem convinced.

"Come now, Evelyn," he said. "I'm sure
she's a very nice little girl. But we can't go
about adopting every nice little girl we come
across."

"But Steven . . ." said the lady.

It was just no good. Mr. Forsythe began to
move toward the door.

"Thank you for your time, Mrs. Crabtree,"

he said. "Come along now, Evelyn. If we hurry we can still catch the evening train."

The lady looked sadly at Amanda then began to put on her bonnet.

Henriette couldn't believe this was happening. Didn't they see that Amanda belonged to them? She had to think of something. Just as the couple reached the door, Henriette turned to Amanda and whispered, "The locket, Amanda. You must show the lady your locket."

None of the grownups heard a sound, but Amanda instantly recognized the tiny voice. She heard it quietly but ever so clearly, floating just above the noise of the traffic in the street. Amanda didn't hesitate. She lifted her chin and said, "Excuse me, ma'am. Would you like to see my locket?"

The lady turned back and said, "What did you say?"

"My locket," said Amanda. "It has a picture of my papa inside."

Amanda handed her locket to the lady in lavender. She sat down on the chair and opened the locket very carefully.

"Oh, Steven. It is Jonathan."

"Let me see that," said Mr. Forsythe.

The lady handed the locket to her husband and said to Amanda, "Where did you get this locket?"

"I've always had it," said Amanda. "Except for the time that Mrs. Crabtree sent it to my grandmother. But then Henriette brought it back to me."

"Who is Henriette?" asked the lady.

"My doll," said Amanda, holding Henriette up for the lady to see.

"She's a very beautiful doll."

"Yes, I know," said Amanda.

"Steven," said the lady, crossing to her husband. "What do you think now?"

"This certainly is a picture of your brother. But it's hardly conclusive. The child could have found the locket anywhere." He handed the locket back to Amanda, then turned to Mrs. Crabtree and said, "You have no other proof of this child's identity?"

"No, I'm sorry," said Mrs. Crabtree.

"Evelyn, we have to think about this. We can't make a decision today. Mrs. Crabtree, we'll be staying at the Grand Hotel. Come along now, Evelyn."

"Good-bye, Amanda," said the lady.

"Good-bye," said Amanda.

The man tipped his hat, took his wife's arm, and led her out the door.

Chapter Fifteen

As soon as the door closed, Mrs. Crabtree turned to Amanda and said, "I'm sorry, Amanda. Perhaps they will change their minds. You may go out and play, but first change your dress."

Amanda walked out of the office and closed the door behind her. She climbed the stairs slowly and went down the hall to the bedroom. Henriette could see that Amanda was very sad.

Henriette's mind was racing. She was determined not to let Mr. and Mrs. Forsythe leave Atlanta without taking Amanda with them. But what could she do? The locket was the only proof they had of Amanda's identity. If only they had found Amanda's grandmother's will. Henriette was certain the will would clear up all these questions.

"I cannot believe my old mistress left no will! If it has not been found, perhaps she hid it somewhere," said Henriette to herself. "Perhaps she was afraid it would fall into the wrong hands. And if it fell into the wrong hands, Amanda might never receive her rightful inheritance. . . ."

Rightful inheritance . . . those words seemed to ring in Henriette's ears as if she had heard them before.

"Ah yes," said Henriette to herself. "Those were the words my old mistress used in the note she sent along with my wardrobe trunk." Henriette closed her eyes and repeated the note word for word:

My Dear Amanda,

You have already received the first part of your rightful inheritance from me . . . and here, safe inside Henriette's trunk, is the rest.

Your loving grandmother,
Amanda Wellington Cartwright
P.S. Tell my oldest friend, Henriette, that I have placed your future in her hands.

"But, of course," exclaimed Henriette. "What a fool I've been!" The note had puzzled Henriette when she read it the first time and now she understood why. It was a kind of secret message. Mrs. Amanda Wellington Cartwright had sent her will to her oldest friend for safekeeping.

Henriette was very excited now. She was certain she knew where to find the proof she needed to convince Mr. Forsythe that Amanda was truly his wife's niece.

That night, just after midnight, Henriette had a meeting of all the dolls from the toy box in the upstairs hallway. She explained the situation concerning Amanda and her aunt and uncle. She told them about the will and the wardrobe trunk. When she finished, Ginger said, "But Henriette, honey, your trunk is down in the cellar."

"Yes, I know," said Henriette.

"So how on earth will you get your hands on it?" asked Ginger. "You-all said yourself Mrs. Crabtree keeps the cellar door locked."

"I will simply have to go the way I went the last time," said Henriette.

"Oh, no, Henriette!" Ginger gasped.

"Don't," warned the Colonel.

"Don't do it," cried Celeste.

All the other dolls protested as well.

"Believe me, my friends," said Henriette, "I do not enjoy the thought of falling once again down the laundry chute, but I see no alternative."

"What will you do once you're down there?" asked the Colonel. "There's no way out of the cellar."

"This is where you are wrong, Colonel Rusticuffs," said Henriette. "I intend to bring the trunk up in the dumbwaiter."

"The dumbwaiter!"

"Really!?"

"You're joking!" said the dolls.

"Colonel," said Henriette, "you yourself told me that it could be done!"

"Yes, I believe I did," said the Colonel. "So I gather you're looking for a rope-and-pulley squad."

"This is correct, Colonel," said Henriette. "I need you and the other dolls to pull the dumbwaiter up when the time comes."

"You're a brave girl, Miss Henriette," said the Colonel. "I'll be glad to help in any way I can."

The other dolls spoke up at once.

"So will I!"

"Me, too!"

"Count me in."

"There's just one thing," said Ginger, who had been quiet for some time. "If you're goin' down the laundry chute, Henriette, I'm comin' with you."

"Oh, no, Ginger," said Henriette. "I could not allow that."

"But how can you move that big trunk all

by yourself? And besides," said Ginger, "I don't see why you should be the only doll around here to have any fun."

"Very well, Ginger," said Henriette. "It would be an honor to have you along."

Then turning to the Colonel she said, "Now, Colonel Rusticuffs, as soon as Ginger and I have gone, you must take all the dolls and stuffed animals down to the kitchen. Stand at the ready and listen for my signal."

"You can count on us," said the Colonel.

"Well, I guess that's it then," said Ginger. "We better get goin', Henriette."

"Yes, of course, Ginger," said Henriette. "Good-bye, my friends."

"Good-bye."

"Good-bye."

All the dolls waved as Henriette and Ginger marched off down the hallway toward the laundry chute.

Chapter Sixteen

WHEN they got to the end of the hall, Ginger opened the little door and looked down the chute.

"Holy cow! It's black as pitch down there."

"It will not be so bad once we're in the cellar," said Henriette. "There are quite a few windows, and the moon is shining brightly tonight."

"It's not that I'm afraid of the dark," said Ginger.

"No, of course not," said Henriette, who was trying with all her might to be brave.

"It's just that I never done nothin' like this before," said Ginger.

"Well, Ginger, I think the time has come." Henriette moved toward the edge of the chute.

"Wait, Henriette," said Ginger. "Let me go first."

"But why?" asked Henriette.

"There's no tellin' what's at the bottom of that chute," said Ginger. "Wash day ain't until next Wednesday."

"This is not your battle, Ginger," said Henriette. "I will go first."

"Use your head, Henriette," said Ginger. "You're a china doll. You may be brave and brainy, but you're made of porcelain. I, on the other hand, am stuffed with corn husks. I go first!"

Henriette started to protest, but Ginger who had moved to the edge of the chute simply said, "See you-all later!" and disappeared.

Henriette gasped. She could hear a wooshing sound as Ginger slid down the long slippery chute, then a dull thud when she hit bottom. Henriette held her breath and waited. After a moment a very small faraway voice said, "C'mon in, Frenchy, the water's fine."

Henriette held her nose, closed her eyes,

and jumped. She slipped and slid feetfirst down the long chute. Her enormous hoopskirt billowed up around her ears as she fell. Henriette made a belly-flop landing into the clothes basket that almost took her breath away. When she opened her eyes, Ginger was standing alongside the basket.

"Happy landings!" said Ginger.

"I believe we have arrived," said Henriette.

They both laughed as Ginger helped Henriette out of the laundry basket.

"Now, where's the trunk?" asked Ginger.

"It is right over here," said Henriette.

The two dolls ran over to the little steamer trunk. Ginger pushed and Henriette pulled until the trunk was out in the middle of the floor. Henriette lifted the lid and said, "You see, Ginger? The lining paper in the lid of the trunk is new. It doesn't match the paper on the sides."

Henriette climbed up onto the edge of the trunk, so she could reach the top of the lid. Ginger steadied the trunk from below. Henriette caught a corner of the paper and, with one sweeping gesture, tore the paper away.

And there Henriette found what she was looking for. Mrs. Cartwright's will had been tucked away in the lid of the trunk. When Henriette tore off the paper lining, the precious document practically fell into her lap.

Henriette opened the will and began to read. It said:

. . . I do bequeath all my earthly goods to my granddaughter Amanda Wellington Conkey, currently residing at the City Orphanage, Atlanta, Georgia. She is the daughter of my beloved daughter Sarah, who married Jonathan Edward Conkey on June 30, 1861 . . .

Henriette didn't read any further. She had all the proof she needed.

"We have found it, Ginger," said Henriette. "Just as I had hoped."

"So what do we do now?" asked Ginger.

"We must move the trunk into the scullery, then find a way to put it into the dumbwaiter."

Ginger took hold of the handle at one end of the trunk and Henriette took the other. On the count of three they lifted together. The trunk was very heavy but Henriette and Ginger were determined dolls. They rested several times along the way, and finally managed to carry the steamer trunk across the cellar floor into the scullery, where they collapsed on top of it, huffing and puffing.

"Now, as I see it, Henriette," said Ginger, "we got to build some kind of staircase."

"My thought exactly," said Henriette. "But what can we use?"

"How about the wooden crates in the other room?" said Ginger. "There's a pile of them next to the washtubs."

"Splendid," said Henriette.

For the next hour or so, the two dolls went back and forth between the laundry room and the scullery, carrying wooden crates. They stacked the wooden crates up and up in front of the dumbwaiter until they made a staircase that reached the compartment. It was only then that Henriette noticed the door to the dumbwaiter was closed.

"Look, Ginger," said Henriette. "What do we do now?"

"Climb up and try to open it," said Ginger.

Ginger climbed the wooden crate staircase very carefully. It creaked and wobbled with each step, but held firm. When she got to the top, she grabbed hold of the handle on the door of the dumbwaiter and pulled up with all her might. It didn't budge.

She turned and looked at Henriette. Suddenly Henriette had an idea. "Ring the bell," she said.

"What's that?" asked Ginger.

"See the bell?" said Henriette pointing just right of Ginger's shoulder. "I think the door will not open if the dumbwaiter is on another floor. You must ring the bell so that the Colonel will send it down to us."

"What if Mrs. Crabtree hears?" asked Ginger.

"That is a chance we will have to take," said Henriette.

So Ginger reached up and gave the bell a short ring. Both dolls held their breath and waited. After a moment they heard the sound of pulleys squeaking. The noise got louder and louder as the dumbwaiter rumbled down the shaft. It arrived with a loud clump.

"Now try the door," said Henriette.

Once again Ginger took hold of the handle and pulled. This time the door slid open.

"*Voilà!* We've done it!" said Henriette to her friend.

Very carefully the two dolls hoisted the trunk up the makeshift staircase. It was hard

work. Henriette had to stop twice to pat her forehead with her pocket handkerchief. Ginger just wiped away the sweat with the back of her hand.

When the trunk was safely stowed inside the dumbwaiter, the two dolls climbed inside and closed the door behind them.

"How do we signal the Colonel?" said Ginger. "The bell is outside."

"I think he will hear if we knock on the sides," said Henriette.

The two dolls rapped sharply on the sides of the compartment, then waited. After a moment, the pulleys began to squeak. The compartment lurched once or twice and then began to rise. Suddenly Henriette remembered the dream she had had several months ago. In the dream she and Ginger had been together in the dumbwaiter. Now that dream was coming true.

Chapter Seventeen

WHEN Mrs. Crabtree came downstairs in the morning, she found Henriette's wardrobe trunk in front of her office door. All the dolls and toys from the toy box were scattered about the floor.

Colonel Rusticuffs and his volunteers had worked on through the night. The dumbwaiter was heavy and hard to lift. The ropes were slippery and very difficult for such tiny hands to grasp.

When the dolls finally succeeded in hauling up the dumbwaiter, Henriette thanked them with all her heart. The dolls were very pleased with themselves. There was a great deal of back-slapping and hand-shaking, but then they realized the task was not done. They had to find a way to get the trunk out of the dumbwaiter and lower it to the ground. The baby doll, Celeste, wanted to push it out and let it fall. But Henriette explained that the trunk was very old and would probably break.

Finally Colonel Rusticuffs found two pieces of rope. Working in teams, the dolls used the ropes to lower the trunk to the floor.

Then Colonel Rusticuffs harnessed the wooden horse to the trunk. The little horse pulled while all the rest of the dolls pushed. Together they managed to move the trunk through the hallways to Mrs. Crabtree's office.

When they finally reached their destination, the Colonel called for a rest break. Exhausted by their efforts, the dolls sat down for just a moment, but one by one they all fell asleep — except for Henriette. She sat on top of the trunk with the precious document clasped tightly in her hands, waiting for morning to come.

When Mrs. Crabtree saw the dolls, she assumed some of the children had gotten up

early to play. She was just about to ring for
the housemaid to take the dolls away when
she noticed that Henriette had something in
her hands. It was a piece of paper folded several
times. It almost seemed as if Henriette were
holding it out for her to see.

Mrs. Crabtree tried to ignore Henriette, but
something about the expression on the doll's
face made it impossible for her to pass. She
hesitated one more moment, then plucked the
piece of paper out of Henriette's hands and
walked into her office.

Henriette watched Mrs. Crabtree out of the
corner of her eye as she sat at her desk and
read the will. She saw Mrs. Crabtree's expres-

sion slowly change as the meaning of the document became clear to her. "Good heavens," said Mrs. Crabtree right out loud. "It's Mrs. Cartwright's will!" Suddenly Mrs. Crabtree stood up and rang for the housemaid.

When Nellie appeared, Mrs. Crabtree said, "Nellie, pick up these dolls and take them upstairs. Then get Amanda up and dressed. See that she puts on her good dress. No, wait, I'll do that. You take this note over to Mr. and Mrs. Steven Forsythe. They are staying at the Grand Hotel. Make sure you give them the note personally. Then go down the street and get old Mr. Plunket, my lawyer. No, wait, never mind. I'll go. You take care of Amanda and the dolls. Well, what are you waiting for?"

Mrs. Crabtree grabbed her hat and cape and ran out the door. It was all Henriette could do to keep from cheering as Nellie picked up an armful of dolls and carried them up the stairs to the dormitory.

Chapter Eighteen

THE day that Henriette and Amanda left the orphanage dawned sunny and bright. Amanda, who had hardly slept at all the night before, was up with the birds. So much had happened so fast that Amanda could hardly believe it.

One moment she was an orphan and the next she was a well-dressed young lady about to set off on a journey to a new home. It had all started when Nellie came running into the room and told her to dress quickly. When she was ready, she had gone down to Mrs. Crabtree's office.

The lady in lavender was there with her husband. There was a great deal of talk about her grandmother and her grandmother's will. Then another man had come into the room. He was a lawyer and his name was Mr. Plunket.

At one point the lady in lavender had knelt down on the floor next to Amanda. She had tears in her eyes, and she said, "Would you like to come home with us, Amanda?" Amanda had hesitated ever so slightly. In that instant Henriette whispered to her, "Tell the lady yes."

The very next morning Mrs. Evelyn Conkey Forsythe had come to get Amanda and Henriette. She took them to lunch at a lovely restaurant. Afterward they went to a dress shop. The lady bought Amanda several new dresses and a small suitcase. She explained that they would be going by train to their new home in Philadelphia.

And so Amanda had risen with the birds. She wanted to be all dressed and waiting when her uncle and aunt came to fetch her. Amanda packed her own little suitcase carefully. Then she had looked through Henriette's wardrobe and selected a blue-and-red plaid traveling costume for her doll. She buttoned the tiny buttons and secured Henriette's hat with a pearl-tipped hat pin.

Amanda and Henriette were ready and waiting when Mrs. Crabtree came into the room. Amanda hugged Molly and Emily, and said good-bye to all the other girls. Everyone wished Amanda good luck, except for Rachel, who stood off in the corner by herself.

Mrs. Crabtree took Amanda's suitcase and the little trunk and said, "Come along, Amanda. It's time to go." Amanda picked up Henriette and started for the door. Just before she left the room she turned to Rachel and said, "Good-bye, Rachel."

At first Rachel didn't say anything. She just stood there, looking at her shoes. But then she smiled and said, "Good-bye, Amanda. I wish you luck."

When Amanda got downstairs, Mr. and Mrs. Forsythe were waiting for her. Mrs. Forsythe took Amanda's hand, and they all walked down the front stairs of the orphanage together.

A carriage was waiting for them at the curb. Mr. Forsythe handed Amanda's suitcase to the

driver, and put Henriette's little trunk inside.
He helped his wife into the carriage, then
lifted Henriette and Amanda up onto the seat.
When they were settled, Mr. Forsythe climbed
in after them and slammed the door.

All the dolls and animals from the toy box
were crowded onto the windowsill of the

orphanage, watching, their faces pressed against the glass. Colonel Rusticuffs saluted Henriette, and Ginger gave her a thumbs-up sign. Henriette looked up at her friends as the carriage drove away, and in her heart she smiled.